Cranky Hazel's

Cake

S K Sheridan

Chapter One

Brainbox Has An Idea!

Cranky Hazel (Young Witch in Training), stared at her cross-eyed cat, Brainbox.

'I'm bored, Brainbox,' she growled. Cranky Hazel *always* growled when she spoke. She NEVER talked in a normal voice and *definitely* never in a soft, giggly little voice. 'Ellie's been away ALL weekend. She's not gonna be back till this afternoon. What in frogs legs am I gonna do till then?' She pushed her spikey black bob behind her ears and crossed her arms. As usual, Agatha and Anton, Cranky Hazel's mum and dad, had put clever-clogs Brainbox in charge that morning before they went up to the attic to conjure up frothing potions and lotions. Apparently they had a back log of orders so would be VERY BUSY today and WERE NOT TO BE DISTURBED.

Brainbox stared back, thinking. At least he stared back with one eye, the other eye was looking in quite the opposite direction, at a toad sitting on a pile of books. Brainbox was exactly the same grey colour as a shadow. This was handy if he didn't want to be found, (like when he fancied a nice, long snooze), because he'd go and lie in a shadowy place

and Cranky Hazel could never spot
him.

A photo of Ellie with her arm
round Cranky Hazel, stood on the
nearby black windowsill in a pink
fluffy frame that Ellie had given her
friend as a birthday present. Pink was
Ellie's favourite colour whereas
Cranky Hazel preferred silvery-black,
although she liked the frame because
Ellie had made it. She glared at the
photo, wishing Ellie was next door
like she usually was at weekends, so
that they could get together and
have some FUN. Having fun was what
Cranky Hazel and Ellie did BEST OF
ALL! Ellie's heart shaped face looked
right back at her, with its sky blue
eyes, freckly nose and the cheekiest

smile in town. Ellie's Mum had taken the photo in the park last year, when Ellie was six and Cranky Hazel was seven.

Cranky Hazel wasn't *always* in a cranky mood, as her grinning photograph face showed. In that picture, even her dark, twinkly eyes were smiling. Ellie loved Cranky Hazel VERY MUCH because she could be kind and funny and did REALLY COOL spells. It was just that certain things, like bossy grownups, awful weather, silly rules, feeling bored and most of all NASTY BULLIES, annoyed Cranky Hazel quite a lot and made her, well, rather cranky and cross. She stuck out her tongue and blew a raspberry at photograph Ellie, then glared back at her cat.

'Well,' Brainbox said eventually, in his EXTREMELY posh voice, when the toad had taken a flying leap onto the dusty floorboards and hopped off. 'Why don't you go and play round at Alfie Fletcher's house. You know he keeps asking you to, and it will be good for you to meet more children your own age while Ellie's not here.' He took a sip of his tea. Brainbox ALWAYS drank tea. He was a very classy cat.

They were in Cranky Hazel's lounge, which her parents had decorated in the traditional witching style. All the walls were painted black with a hint of grey. Spider's webs (both real and plastic) hung from every corner. A rusty cauldron bubbled away in the fire place, a brown stew in it filling the air with spicy smells. A row of multi-coloured bottles stood on a shelf and underneath them sat a pile of books, (now minus the toad), that had titles like, "How To Turn Toads Into Gold", "A Witch's Guide to Humans", and "Cauldron Meals For Dummies". The sofa and arm chair were grey, torn and hard, which was EXACTLY how Cranky Hazel and her parents liked them.

'Eugh, YUK,' Cranky Hazel growled. 'I DON'T WANT to get to know other children. They're so dull and smelly. I just want Ellie to come back. She must be HATING every minute of her weekend, being stuck with those bossy parents of hers at her grandparents' house. Hey,' she said, straightening up, pushing her ragged witch's hat up. It had got stuck on her one, small wart, which stuck up on the end of her nose. Cranky Hazel was VERY proud of that wart.

'I've just had the most AMAZEBALLS idea. If Ellie can't be with us here, we should go to HER. She'll probably be really missin' us by now, and she might need rescuin' from her ridiculous mother.' Cranky Hazel grinned triumphantly.

Brainbox sighed and closed the book he'd been reading with his paw.

'Don't you think Mr and Mrs Morgan might object if you and I suddenly turn up at Ellie's grandparent's house unannounced?' He said. 'They've probably been looking forward to a peaceful weekend ON THEIR OWN for ages.'

'A weekend of bossin' poor Ellie around more like,' Cranky Hazel growled. 'Alright then clever clogs. If we can't go and visit her what CAN we do? I've already counted my wands, rusted the cauldron, fed the spiders, toads and mice, polished my hat, rearranged my stripy stockings and practised my broom flying, not to mention makin' you hundreds of boilin' hot cups of tea. What else is there to do? She won't be home for HOURS.'

Brainbox looked up at the ceiling and blinked three times.

'I've got an idea,' he said, sitting up. 'Why don't you make her a welcome home cake? That will keep you busy for a while.'

'Good idea,' Cranky Hazel growled, jumping up. 'I'll go and magic one up in the kitchen.'

'Oh no, you can't do that,' Brainbox said quickly. 'Ellie is a *human* not a witch. You'll have to make the cake the HUMAN way.'

'Eh?' Cranky Hazel stopped and scratched her head. 'How do you do that then?'

Brainbox rolled his eyes in different directions.

'By going to the supermarket, buying the ingredients, mixing them together, pouring the mixture into a tin, then baking it in the oven,' he said.

'OK,' Cranky Hazel growled, stamping off over the cracked floorboards. 'Fine. Then that's what I'll do, it sounds easy peasy. And it will be the BEST cake Ellie's ever tasted, so there.' She disappeared out of the door then stuck her head back through. 'Are you coming or not?' She growled. 'I've never been to the supermarket before. This could be fun!'

'Oh dear,' Brainbox sighed, standing up and stretching. 'I'm having second thoughts about this plan already.'

Chapter Two

Trouble At The Park

'Come on, keep up,' Cranky Hazel growled over her shoulder. She was stamping along the pavement, her legs wide apart, her hobnailed boots crunching over the concrete. Cranky Hazel ALWAYS walked like that. She never walked normally, and CERTAINLY never in a dainty way.

She'd rather eat her own boots that do that.

'I'm coming,' Brainbox said, sauntering along behind her, tail held high. 'Shall we take the short cut through the park?'

'Yeah alright,' Cranky Hazel growled, swinging left through the two high park gates. She stamped off down the path that led round the duck pond and over the bridge, Brainbox padding along behind her all the time.

'Ooh look at that,' Cranky Hazel pointed to a lush, green blanket of grass laid out in front of her. A low, white fence ran all the way around it. She stared at the bouncy moss and the beautiful flowers poking up here and there all over the grass. Cranky Hazel loved running across grass and she loved smelling beautiful flowers, they were two of her most favourite things to do EVER. 'That looks MUCH more fun to walk on than this stony path. Look how soft and squishy it is. Come on Brainbox, follow me!'

'Remember what happened last time,' the cat called, but it was too late. Cranky Hazel hitched up her robes, jumped over the fence and stomped over the bouncy, mossy grass.

'Yippee!' She cackled. 'This is fun.' She breathed in deeply, enjoying the fresh smells. 'Delicious,' she shouted as she smelt a rose. 'Yummy,' she cackled as she sniffed a geranium. Brainbox watched, his eyebrows raised, as Cranky Hazel danced around the daisies, jigged around the jasmine and trotted around the tulips, cackling all the time. Young witches loved perfecting their cackle, and Cranky Hazel practised hers a lot, mostly at bed time or in the shower.

Mr Perkins the park keeper looked up from the recycling bin he was emptying. He took the park rule book EXTREMELY seriously and had spent a long time learning it off by heart. He'd met Cranky Hazel before, he remembered, possibly around this time last year, and it hadn't gone well. He cleared his throat, but Cranky Hazel didn't take any notice.

'Hey,' he yelled, reaching for his whistle. 'Hey you, little witchy in the pointy hat. Can't you see the sign? It says, "Please Do *Not* Walk On The Grass".' He pointed at a small white sign stuck into one corner of the lawn.

Cranky Hazel stopped stomping and stared at him.

'What is the point,' she growled loudly. 'Of growin' grass in a park if you can't even walk on it? It's like taking a van full of ice creams to the beach then not selling any to hungry children. It's ridiculous and it doesn't make sense.'

'It's important grass,' Mr Perkins said, puffing his chest out as far as he could as he marched towards her. He didn't know WHY it was important grass, but it must be if there was a sign saying not to walk on it. Signs meant a lot to Mr Perkins. 'It can't be disturbed. Not even *I* am allowed to walk on it.'

'Well that's just really SILLY then isn't it?' Cranky Hazel growled loudly, standing her ground.

Brainbox sighed and waited. This was exactly what had happened last year. He reflected that in future, Cranky Hazel better stick to the playground area at the other end of the park. She and Ellie went there a lot with Ellie's mum after her friend got back from school. Sometimes Brainbox came along if he had nothing better to do, so he knew that

Ellie and Cranky Hazel had great fun going on the slide, swings, roundabout, climbing frame and seesaw together as well as playing hide and seek behind the tall trees and wide bushes. (That is until Cranky Hazel got over tired and started ZAPPING things with her wand, and had to be led home in a mood for dinner and bed). Things did not tend to go so well at THIS end of the park.

'GET OFF THE GRASS,' Mr Perkins shouted, his face flushing purple. 'If you don't get off now, I'll blow my whistle.'

Cranky Hazel rolled her eyes.

'Ooh no,' she said. 'Not the whistle. Anythin' but the whistle.'

She did a little jig next to the jasmine, kicking the edge of her robes into the air and flashing her stripy green and black stockings.

'Right, that's IT,' Mr Perkins yelled, trembling. He was sure the rule book DEFINITELY said no jigging next to the jasmine. He stuffed the whistle into his mouth and blew hard.

'PHEEEEEEEEEE!'

'Ooh, that's a horrible noise,' Cranky Hazel growled, putting her hands over her ears. 'Come on Brainbox, let's go. I've had enough of it here. We've got more important things to do, like buy ingredients for Ellie's welcome home cake.' She stomped off towards the path, her cat following and watching as she reached deep into her robe pocket and pulled out her wand.

A little backwards flick of her wrist sent an arc of CRACKLING black and silver whistle shapes shooting into the air towards Mr Perkins.

'Whoops,' she cackled, as his park keeper's hat flew off and got stuck high up in a tree. 'I think my wand slipped.'

'Cranky Hazel,' Brainbox said, shaking his head. A smile seemed to have spread across his feline face. 'You've *got* to behave yourself from now on. No more shenanigans and *definitely* none in the supermarket. Look, that's the gate we need.' He pointed to a small gate set between a greenhouse and a wall with his paw.

'Come on then, keep up,' she growled, stamping towards it down the gravelly path.

'Where's my hat?' Mrs Perkins shouted.

Cranky Hazel cackled as she slammed the gate behind her.

Chapter Three

Supermarket Adventure

Cranky Hazel had been jumping backwards and forwards through the automatic doors of the supermarket for four and a half minutes.

'Come on, let's go,' Brainbox said sternly. 'If we stay here any longer the cake won't be made and baked by the time Ellie gets back.'

'This is fun,' she cackled, ignoring him. A man in a smart suit took one look at what Cranky Hazel was doing, then stuck his nose in the air and walked away, tutting. Cranky Hazel ignored HIM too. She never cared what ANYONE thought about her. 'What great doors,' she growled. 'I want some. Where do you think they'd look best? In Granny's lounge?'

'Don't even THINK about it,' Brainbox said, imagining the whole house full of automatic doors and shaking his head.

'Alright spoilsport,' Cranky Hazel jumped through into the supermarket one last time and picked up a basket. She stared at the aisles in front of her, with their signs and brightly wrapped assorted packets, tins and bottles. 'Wowzers, what a lot of food! I LOVE it here, I bet they even sell pickled seaweed, which as you know, is my very favourite snack. Come on then. What do we need first?'

'Butter,' Brainbox stalked off. 'You always need butter when you're making a cake.'

'What about baked beans?' Cranky Hazel growled, as they passed a high stack of tins. 'Ellie LOVES baked beans. I think I'll put some of them in the cake.' She threw a tin into the basket.

'No,' Brainbox said. 'DEFINITELY not. No one eats baked bean cakes.'

'Well Ellie's not a no one. She's a SOME ONE,' Cranky Hazel growled. The tin of baked beans remained in the basket.

'Cheese?' Cranky Hazel suggested, as they passed a fridge full of different coloured cheeses. 'Ellie loves cheese. I think we'll put some of that in.'

Brainbox groaned.

'We're not making a cheesecake,' he sighed. But Cranky

Hazel picked up a huge lump of orange cheese and heaved it into the basket.

'There,' she growled. 'That looks tasty.'

'There's the butter,' Brainbox pointed. 'You need a tub of that.' Cranky Hazel chucked the biggest one she could find into the basket.

'That should be enough, I reckon,' she growled.

'Ah, here's the baking aisle,' Brainbox said as they rounded a corner. 'Look, there are the eggs.' He pointed to rows of fragile looking cardboard boxes.

'How many eggs do we need? About thirty?' Cranky Hazel asked.

'Just get a pack of six,' Brainbox said. 'But check inside to make sure none of them are broken before you put the box in the basket.'

Cranky Hazel grabbed a box by the lid and lifted it up. All the eggs slid out and smashed on top of her hob nailed boots, leaving a yellow, crunchy puddle oozing all around her.

'Whoops,' she cackled, as Brainbox rolled his eyes and looked over his shoulder. No one else was in the baking aisle. Cranky Hazel reached for her wand and with a flick of her wrist sent tiny chicken shaped glitter balls CHEEPING all over the eggy mess. They sucked up the mess like sponges then disappeared.

'Try again,' Brainbox said. 'But this time, BE CAREFUL. Hold the box with both hands.'

Cranky Hazel grabbed a box of eggs with one hand and opened the lid with the other. Six perfect eggs sat in two rows of three.

'Yep,' she growled, closing the box and putting it in her basket on top of the butter. 'These ones will do. Now what?'

'Sugar and icing sugar,' Brainbox pointed at some different sized bags. Cranky Hazel picked up two and chucked them on top of the baked beans. 'And flour,' Brainbox pointed to another shelf. 'Get self-raising flour.'

'Alright, bossy-boots,' Cranky Hazel stamped over and chose a big bag and heaved it into the basket. It was now so full it was becoming a bit difficult to pick up.

'Now let's go and pay,' Brainbox said, turning.

On the way to the tills, Cranky Hazel added chocolate chip biscuits, frozen chunky chips and a packet of sausages to the basket.

'I think we have all the ingredients for our cake now,' she growled, slamming the basket on to the next free counter.

'Did you find everything you were looking for today, young lady?'

The shop assistant asked as he beeped each item through.

'No,' Cranky Hazel growled. 'I was lookin' for pickled seaweed and you don't seem to have any. It's my favourite snack and I haven't had any for ages.'

'Ah,' the shop assistant's brow crinkled. 'No, ah, I don't think we sell, er, pickled seaweed.'

'Oh,' Cranky Hazel growled, her bottom lip sticking out.

'Um,' the shop assistant said. 'That will be nine pounds and seventy six pence, please.'

Cranky Hazel took off her witch's hat and shook it. A bulging purse fell out on to the counter. (Her parents, who were always busy making potions and lotions to sell so they could pay the electricity bill, left a steady supply of money out for Cranky Hazel and Brainbox, just in case they ran out of bread or toothpaste or chocolate or something else important). Cranky Hazel grabbed her purse, undid the zip, and counted out the right money, slamming each coin down on the counter HARD.

'There!' She growled when she'd finished.

'Thank you,' the shop assistant said faintly, handing Cranky Hazel her bag of shopping. 'Have a nice day.'

Chapter Four

Bully Boy

'Shall we walk through the park again?' Cranky Hazel asked, stomping along, swinging her bag of shopping. 'I could whizz Mr Perkin's hat even higher this time.'

'No, I don't think so,' Brainbox said hurriedly. 'I think we better go home the *long* way. It will do us both good to get a bit of exercise.'

'Oh OK,' Cranky Hazel growled, and stamped off at a fast pace down a street lined with houses.

'Doo-bee-doo-bee-dooh,' she growl-sang, as they walked along past fences, cars and trees, Brainbox padding along next to her. Cranky Hazel liked singing A LOT and her favourite television programme was "The Witch Factor", which was a singing competition. She thought she might enter when she was older. Brainbox wasn't sure about THAT idea but he was too polite to say anything.

A movement in one of the front garden's caught her eye. Cranky Hazel stopped and stared.

'Hmm,' she growled.

Two brothers were standing in one of the front gardens, watching their dad slosh soapy water over his car, then rub the side of the car with a sponge. The big boy, who had stubbly brown hair, munched down the last bit of his ice cream cone, wiped his mouth with the back of his hand, then looked over at his little brother, who had longer, curly brown hair. The smaller boy was licking his nearly WHOLE ice cream slowly, obviously enjoying every little bit of it. The big boy checked to see where his father was, which happened to be round the other side of the car, then snatched the ice cream out of his brother's hand. In three snorting munches, he'd finished the whole lot.

'Hey, that's not right,' Cranky Hazel growled under her breath, and Brainbox shook his head from side to side, tutting. If there was one thing Cranky Hazel HATED MOST in life, it was a BULLY!

It took the young boy a couple of seconds to take in what had happened. Then he looked up at his brother and opened his mouth. Brainbox braced himself for an ear splitting scream, but Cranky Hazel had an idea. She quickly flicked her wand, and a mass of ice cream cone shaped glitter stars WHOOSHED over the little boy, who suddenly found he was holding the LARGEST, STICKIEST most AMAZING ice cream he'd ever seen in his LIFE. Red, pink, blue and yellow scrummy ice cream balls sat in a chocolate wafer cone. Toffee fudge sauce with marshmallow pieces on top of it oozed down the sides of the ice cream in yummy rivers. It was much better than the boring vanilla ice cream his brother had just nicked from him.

'Wow,' shouted the boy.

The elder boy blinked twice, then reached for his brother's new ice cream.

'Dad,' shouted the young boy, ready for it the second time round. 'Darren's trying to steal my ice cream.'

'Darren, leave your brother alone,' the dad said, sticking his head round the side of the car so he could see what was going on. 'I'm sick of you picking on him. Do something useful for once, come here and help me wash the car.'

Cranky Hazel cackled under her breath as the little boy sat down on the doorstep, enjoying his GIANT ice cream in peace, as the elder one stomped towards the soapy car, his face as moody as a thunder cloud. None of them noticed the little witch and shadowy grey cat watching them.

'Come on,' Brainbox said, an unmistakeable grin beneath his whiskers. 'We'd better go. If we don't hurry up a bit we won't have time to make the cake before Ellie gets back.'

'Fine,' Cranky Hazel cackled, and stamped off down the road, swinging the bag of shopping. With a flick of his tail, Brainbox turned and followed her.

Chapter Five

How To Make A Cake

'Tie my apron up at the back please, Brainbox,' Cranky Hazel growled. She was standing next to her black kitchen counter, staring at the row of ingredients. Black kitchen scales, a grey mixing bowl, a rusty cake tin and a dark brown wooden spoon lay behind them. Brainbox padded behind her and tied a neat bow with his paws.

'I've already told you we don't need the baked beans, cheese, chocolate biscuits, chips and sausages to make the cake,' he said, jumping on to the counter.

'Are you a silly ninny or somethin'?' Cranky Hazel growled. 'How many times do I have to tell you that baked beans, cheese, chocolate biscuits, chips and sausages are ELLIE'S FAVOURITE FOODS. I bet she'd be really upset if I didn't put them in her cake.'

'Fine,' Brainbox said. 'I tell you what, you make Ellie a cake YOUR way and I'll make Ellie a cake MY way. Agreed?'

'Alright Mr Smarty Pants,' Cranky Hazel growled. 'You're on.'

Brainbox reached up, opened the cupboard and got down another mixing bowl, cake tin and wooden spoon. He reached forwards, picked up the butter and measured out four ounces of it in the scales. Cranky Hazel grabbed the tub and spooned the rest of it into her bowl. Then she sloshed the whole tin of baked beans in as well.

'Ooh,' She cackled. 'Ellie's goin' to love this. Now what?'

'Eggs,' Brainbox said, daintily cracking two into his bowl, then throwing the shells in the bin.

Cranky Hazel grabbed the box and smashed the four remaining eggs into her bowl, sending yoke, egg white and bits of shell flying all over the kitchen. She stared at the bowl with her head on one side, then picked up the packet of chocolate biscuits, threw it on the floor and stamped on it, CRUNCH! CRUNCH! She picked up the now floppy packet and emptied the biscuit bits into her mixing bowl.

'There,' she growled, wiping her hands on her apron. 'That looks more like it.'

Brainbox picked up his spoon and stirred his butter and eggs together carefully. Cranky Hazel grabbed her spoon and stirred her eggs, baked beans, butter and bits of biscuits together really fast, pretending she was an electric whisk. WHIZZ WHIZZ. Bits of the gloopy, crunchy mixture splattered out over Cranky Hazel's face.

'Whoops!' She screeched. 'This mixin' is hurtin' my arm, Brainbox. Can't I just use magic for this bit?'

'No,' he said, sternly. 'Ellie's cake has to be made the HUMAN way from start to finish, or she might not like it.'

'Fine,' Cranky Hazel snapped, her arm whizzing even faster. After two minutes she stopped, panting, and slammed the wooden spoon down on to the counter. 'Now what?'

'Watch me,' Brainbox said, as he measured out four ounces of sugar in the scales then carefully poured the white granules on top of his mixture.

'Easy peasy lemon squeezy,' Cranky Hazel cackled, and tipped the rest of the sugar into her bowl. Then she stared at the bowl with her hands on her hips for a few seconds. 'Hang on a minute,' she growled. 'It needs a little somethin' extra.' She opened the bag of frozen chips and chucked in four handfuls. 'That should do it.'

Brainbox raised his eyes to the ceiling, then picked up the bag of self-raising flour.

'Now,' he said. 'We measure out four ounces of flour.' He picked up the big bag.

'Come on, hurry up slow coach,'
Cranky Hazel drummed her foot on
the floor waiting for him to finish. As
soon as he did, she seized the bag
and emptied the flour into her bowl
so fast it came out in a puffy cloud
that turned her face and witch's hat
completely white.

'PAH!' She yelled, rubbing her
hand across her eyes. 'Yuk! Bakin'
the human way is REALLY MESSY!
Now what?'

'Now we stir the mixture again,'
Brainbox said, picking up his spoon.
He stirred his until it was creamy and
smooth.

Cranky Hazel picked up her
spoon and stirred the chips, flour and
sugar into the biscuit bits, eggs,

baked beans and butter. Her mixture was chunky, bumpy and multi coloured.

'Yum yum,' she licked her lips. 'Mine looks MUCH better than yours.'

'If you say so,' Brainbox said. He pulled a cake tin towards him with his paw, then poured his mixture into it.

Cranky Hazel watched, then poured HER mixture into the other cake tin. Then she opened the packet of sausages and stood them upright like soldiers throughout the tin, then laid chunks of cheese all over the top of them.

'Hurray,' she cackled, standing back and staring at the finished product. 'Mine's a BEAUTIFUL work of art. Don't feel bad that yours looks so BORIN', Brainbox.'

'Yes, er, righto,' Brainbox said, looking at his smooth mixture proudly.

'So how do we bake the cakes then?' Cranky Hazel growled. 'We can't use the cauldron, Mum's stew's still cookin' and we're goin' to eat that later for dinner. Shall I do a bakin' spell?' She reached for her wand.

'NO,' Brainbox shouted, holding out his paw. 'We need to use the oven.'

'Oh right,' Cranky Hazel growled, scratching her head, looking round her kitchen. 'I didn't know we had one.'

When both cake tins were on the top shelf of the oven and Brainbox had turned the dial to the right temperature, Cranky Hazel pulled a chair in front of the oven and sat down.

'I'm not movin' till it's ready,' she growled, leaning forwards. Brainbox chuckled, then turned to start the washing up.

Chapter Six

Ellie Judges The Cakes

Cranky Hazel hopped from one foot to the other while Brainbox slowly opened the oven door. They stared at the two VERY different creations inside. One was smooth, round and golden. The other had completely EXPLODED out of the cake tin; burnt cheese sat smoking on top of brown sausages, which protruded from a lumpy sea of baked beans, crispy chips, over-cooked biscuit bits and fluffy sponge cake. It looked like something you might expect to find at the bottom of a dustbin.

'Oh Cranky Hazel, I'm SO sorry –
' Brainbox began.

'Its – its PERFECT!' Cranky Hazel
shouted, clapping her hands. 'I've
never seen such a SCRUMPTIOUS
lookin' cake in my life. Sorry yours
didn't turn out very interestingly,'
she raised her eyes at Brainbox's
sponge cake.

Brainbox opened his mouth,
then shut it again.

'Right.' He said. 'Yes.
Absolutely. Yours does indeed look,
er, unbelievable.'

While Brainbox mixed up some
white icing and Cranky Hazel was
admiring her cake, Ellie's face
appeared at the kitchen window.

'Ellie!' Cranky Hazel cackled, going over to open the back door. 'You're back. Did you have a completely horrible time at your grandparent's house without me?'

'Of course I did,' Ellie said, flinging her arms around her friend and giving her a tight squeeze. 'It would have been MUCH better if you'd been there. Ooh, what's that funny smell?'

'That,' Cranky Hazel growled. 'Is what the AMAZIN' surprise I just made for you smells like.'

'I like surprises,' Ellie said, trying to peer round Cranky Hazel. What is it, can I see?'

'Perhaps,' Brainbox said quickly as he deftly smoothed icing all over his cake with a knife. 'We should just explain to Ellie that we BOTH made our OWN versions of the surprise.'

'Ooh, two surprises, even better,' Ellie laughed.

Cranky Hazel cleared her throat.

'Brainbox and I,' she growled. 'Have both made you Welcome Home cakes, because we missed you so much this weekend. Brainbox tried hard but mine's definitely the best.'

She stepped aside. Brainbox slid his perfectly iced cake back next to Cranky Hazel's mountainous one.

Ellie's mouth fell open as she stared from one to the other. She took in the smooth, round edges, the careful icing and the flat, circular top of Brainbox's cake. Then she stared at the higgledy piggledy eruption of sausages, chips, baked beans, biscuit bits and cheese amid mountains of fluffy sponge cake that made up Cranky Hazel's cake.

'I think,' she said, concentrating hard and not looking at either Cranky Hazel or Brainbox. 'That they are BOTH perfect cakes in different ways.'

Brainbox grinned, then stalked off towards the cutlery drawer.

Cranky Hazel nudged Ellie.

'Mine's really your favourite isn't it?' She growl-whispered as Brainbox pulled out a knife.

'Yes,' Ellie whispered back. 'Yours is amazing. No one's EVER made me a cake with ALL my favourite food in it before! Thank you very much, it was a wonderful idea.'

'Yes it was, wasn't it,' Cranky Hazel growled, looking pleased.

'Who's would you like a slice of first?' Brainbox said, his eyes gleaming.

'Ooh, pick mine, pick mine,' Cranky Hazel shrieked.

'I think,' Ellie said. 'That yours is just TOO beautiful to eat, Cranky

Hazel. Perhaps we could all have a slice of Brainbox's?'

'Of course,' Brainbox said, holding the knife with his paw and cutting his cake up while Cranky Hazel took three black side plates out of the cupboard. 'It would be my pleasure.' He carefully placed three big slices on the three plates.

So then Ellie, Cranky Hazel and Brainbox munched away in the black and grey kitchen while real and fake spider webs hung above their heads, discussing how brilliant the cakes were between mouthfuls.

A little bit later, Ellie's mum Claire, (who wasn't NEARLY as bossy as Cranky Hazel thought she was), came round to see how everything was going and to say that dinner was nearly ready. Ellie asked her mum to take a photo of Cranky Hazel's cake with her phone, which she did, saying she'd print the photo out when she had time so that Ellie always had a picture of the AMAZING "Welcome Home" cake her best friend had made specially for her.

Cranky Hazel got into her long, thin bed and pulled up her black and grey stripy duvet VERY HAPPILY that night, pleased that her best friend Ellie was back next door, and EXTREMELY pleased that she'd made her such an AMAZIN' welcome home cake. She was looking forwards to the fun they'd have the next day when Ellie came home from school, because after all, having fun was what Cranky Hazel and Ellie did best. Brainbox curled up on top of Cranky Hazel's feet and within minutes the pair of them were fast asleep, both dreaming of baking cakes...THE HUMAN WAY!

Printed in Great Britain
by Amazon